Jim Henson's™

THE

Hoobs™

£5.99
UK only

HOOBY CONTENTS

HUBBA HUBBA

Hoobledoop Tiddlypeeps!

Welcome to the hoobledoobledooper Hoobs Annual – packed with hoobloads of hoobygroovy stories and hoobashious fun for Tiddlypeeps. It's fantabihooby!

I've sent four of my hoobygrooviest Hoobs to learn all about your Peep planet for my Hoobopaedia.

Look out, here they come...

"Hoobledoop Tiddlypeeps! We're the Hoobs! Iver, Tula, Groove and Roma!"

TULA

"Every Hoob day begins with a question. And every question needs an answer! Sometimes we need help and then we ask YOU – the Tiddlypeeps – our clever friends!"

IVER

"Once we find the answer, we report back using hoobytechnology to Hubba Hubba in Hoobland and he puts all the answers into his great Hoobopaedia!"

"There are lots of questions and answers to read about in this hoobashious annual – so read on and have a hoobygroovy time!"

6

You know who the Hoobs are
Iver, Groove and Tula
We're Hoobs!
And we're ready to go

Now the wheels are turning
We can all get learning
All the things we want to know

Hubba Hubba's in Hoobland
And Roma's somewhere far away
The Motorettes are singing
The engine keeps on spinning

Hoob, Hoob, Hooray!

The Hoobmobile is coming your way
The Hoobs are here
So what do you say?

HOOBS!

Here's a hooby hello from
GROOVE

"Hoobledoop! Hoobledoop! Whoop! Whoop! Whoop!"

"Hoobledoop Tiddlypeeps. I'm Groove. I have green hoobyfur, a green twizzletuft (that's hair in peep speak) and a red nose! I love to collect things. And I love giving hoobprepa diggers to the other Hoobs! Hoobprepa diggers are hoobygroovy!"

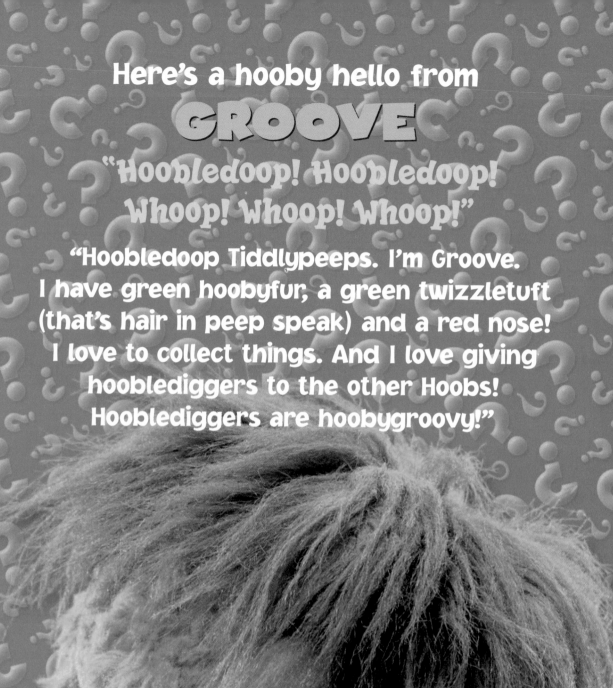

groove

8

A hoobashious picture of Groove for you to colour.

JUICIEST FRUIT

One day, inside the Hoobmobile...

Tula was building a hoobelly groobelly apple tower. But, while she wasn't looking, along came Groove, who took a huge, juicy bite!

"Groove! That was my biggest, juiciest apple," scolded Tula. "Sorry!" said Groove. "To make it up to you, I will find an even bigger, juicier fruit to go on top of your tower! In fact I will find the biggest, juiciest fruit in whole Peep world."

"Which is the biggest, juiciest Peep fruit in the world?"

"I've checked the Hoobnet and there are lots of Peep fruits," said Hubba Hubba. "Do you know their names?"

"Hoobygalooby!" said Tula. "I never knew there were so many kinds of Peep fruit. We'd better ask the Tiddlypeeps for some help!"

"Yeah!" agreed Groove. "Let's get those Motorettes singing!"

We're off to see
the Tiddlypeeps,
On the road we go!
We're off to see
the Tiddlypeeps,
They're smart,
They're fun,
They know!

The Tiddlypeeps,
The Tiddlypeeps!
Help us find things out!
They give us clues,
They tell us the news,
That's what they're all about!

The Tiddlypeeps,
The Tiddlypeeps!
If we need to know,
Who, what, where,
Why, when and how,
We'll ask them,
off we go!

It was half time at the Tiddlypeeps' football match and they were enjoying a plate of orange slices.

Groove decided that an orange must be the biggest, juiciest fruit. Iver wasn't so sure. "An orange isn't that much bigger than an apple," he said, holding the two fruits up next to each other.

Back at the Hoobmobile, Roma checked in with her daily news report: "Hoobledoop, Hoobs. I've come all the way to Africa today, to a place called a plantation where pineapples grow! They are spiky on the outside but inside they are hoobashiously juicy! Not only that Hoobs, but they're big, big, BIG! And they even have their own twizzletuft just like a Hoob! **Hoobletoodledoo!**"

"I think the pineapple must be the biggest, juiciest fruit in the Peep world!" said Groove.

"Me too," said Tula. "Let's order a whole box of pineapples so I can make an even bigger fruit tower!"

"I'm off to a Tiddlypeep tea-party," said Groove, "I'll take a pineapple with me..."

But when Groove arrived, he found one of the Tiddlypeeps eating something even bigger and juicier than his pineapple!

It was a watermelon!

He took one back to the Hoobmobile for Tula.

"But how am I going to put it on top of my fruit tower?" she asked.

"You can't!" said Groove.

"OK. I have a better idea," laughed Tula. "I'll eat it!" And off she ran!

Give me a fruit
That I can toot
A noisy fruit
Would be a hoot
A juicy fruit
Is just the thing

The biggest one
Of which we sing
Oh clever Hoobs
We've got to
tell 'em

Is the most hoobashious
WATERMELON!

A HOOBY PUZZLE

Can you count how many apples Tula has in her fruit tower?

Draw some more fruit for her.

Make a
FRUITY HOOB

You will need:
One Peep
One big, juicy pineapple
Two cherries or grapes
One kiwi fruit
One small orange
Five cocktail sticks

1 Ask your Peep to slice the bottom from the pineapple and stand it on a plate.

2 Make two hooby eyes using grapes or cherries. Cocktail sticks will keep them in place.

3 Make two hooby ears from your orange and one hoobashious nose from your kiwi fruit.

4 Now give your Hoob a hooby groovy name!

17

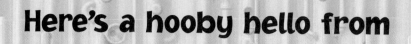

Here's a hooby hello from
IVER

"Hoobledoop! Hoobledoop! Whoop! Whoop! Whoop!"

"Hoobledoop Tiddlypeeps. I'm Iver. I have purple hoobyfur, a green twizzletuft and a green nose! I'm always bouncy and full of energy – and sometimes the other Hoobs have to remind me to take it easy!"

A hoobelly groobelly picture of Iver for you to colour.

One day, inside the Hoobmobile...

Groove was feeling lonely. "I've been out collecting things by myself all day," he said, sadly.

"Poor Groove," said Tula. "We must find someone to keep you company, but who?"

Just then, Hubba Hubba appeared on the hoobycomputer screen. "Hoobledoop, Hoobs," he said. "That's a hoobashious question for my Hoobopaedia!"

"Who could keep Groove company while he's out collecting things?"

Here are some animals that might keep Groove company. Do you know their names?

Roar! Roar!

Bounce! Bounce!

Croak! Croak!

Snap! Snap!

"Would you like any of those to keep you company, Groove?" asked Tula. "The stick insect!" said Groove. "He reminds me of my favourite pencil!"

"Hmmm, I'm not sure," said Tula. "He looks a bit small and if you put him in your pocket he might get squished!"

Just then, Hubba Hubba found a story about pets on the Hoobnet...

There was once a little boy called Percy who loved the sound of his own voice.

One day Percy's mum bought him the perfect pet; a parrot. But Percy didn't understand.

"I don't really like feathers.

I'm not that keen on beaks.

And watching things fly makes me feel funny.

The only thing I like is the sound of my own voice. So why is a parrot the perfect pet for me?"

"Well, why don't you ask it?" said his mum.
And so Percy did.

"Why are you the perfect pet for me?" asked Percy.
"Why are you the perfect pet for me?" repeated the parrot.

"You just said what I said!" said Percy. "You just said what I said!" said the parrot. "Are you going to say everything I say?" asked Percy. "Are you going to say everything I say?" said the parrot.

And then Percy smiled. Suddenly he knew why the parrot was the most perfect pet for him... because it would always say exactly what he said!

"Now I've got you, I can hear the sound of my own voice all day long," said Percy.

"Now I've got you, I can hear the sound of my own voice all day long," said the parrot.

"I love you!" said Percy.
"I love you!" said the
parrot!

THE END

"Let's ask the Tiddlypeeps who could keep Groove company," said Iver, "they know lots of things and they really love animals!"

So they all jumped into the Hoobmobile, and whizzed off to visit the Tiddlypeeps.

"Animals are our pets!" explained the Tiddlypeeps. "They keep us company and we look after them. Look – here's Hoppy!"

"Why is he called that?" asked Groove.

"Because that's what he does!" laughed the Tiddlypeeps.

"I like him!" said Groove. "He has a very twitchy nose!"

One of the Tiddlypeeps had a different kind of pet.

"His name is Chunky. He has four legs, a swishy tail and he lives in a stable. Do you know what he is?"

Groove, Iver and Tula couldn't guess. Can you?

"He's a pony!" said the Tiddlypeeps. "You have to muck out his stable every week!"

"Yuk!" said Groove. "Sounds too whiffy for me! What other animals make good pets?"

"What? What? What?" sang the Motorettes.

One of the Tiddlypeeps had a dog. "A dog can be your best friend! But you have to think of a good name for him and throw sticks for him to fetch!"

Groove thought it sounded fun so he tried – again, and again and again! "Doesn't the dog ever get tired?" he sighed. "Oh dear. I'm never going to find the right pet to keep me company. A rabbit is too hoppy. A parrot is too talky. A pony is too whiffy and a dog is too fetchy!" He looked at the stick he was holding and had an idea. "I know!" he said. "This stick can be my pet! He's like a stick insect, but bigger! He won't **hop**, he won't **talk**, he won't **whiff** and he won't **fetch**! He's perfect! And guess what I'm going to call him – **Sticky**!"

Woof! Woof!

27

WHO LIVES WHERE?

Just as the Hoobs live in their hoobygroovy Hoobmobile, so animals have their own favourite places to live.

Can you guess which animals might live in these hoobashious animal homes?

BABY ANIMALS

Little Peeps are called Tiddlypeeps (or Squigglytiddlypeeps if they are hoobashiously small). Little animals have special names too. How many of these baby animals can you name? (If you don't know the name, make one up!)

MAKE HOPPY EARS

You can pretend to be a fluffy, twitchy rabbit like the Hoobs by making your own rabbit ears...

You will need:

A large white paper plate
Scissors
Crayons, paints or felt pens
A stapler
A Peep to help you

1 Ask your Peep to cut the middle from the paper plate. (Tell them to try to keep the centre piece intact as you will need it later.)

The circle you are left with is your headband and it sits on your head and behind your ears.

Try it on for size.

2 Cut two ears from the centre piece and use your crayons, paints or pens to decorate them.

3 Ask your Peep to use the stapler to attach the ears to the headband.

4 If you have face-paints at home, you can give yourself whiskers and a twitchy rabbit nose too!

Now all you have to do is ...

hop! hop! hop! hop!

You can make other animal ears in the same way! How many other animals can you pretend to be? See how many different animal noises you can make!

What's on the
HOOB MENU?

Here's everything a Hoob would love to eat!
Colour it in to make it look even more delicious!

Hoobygoop –
a sweet sticky syrup

Hoobybun –
a green bun

Hoobnips – a hooby
vegetable

Hoobofizz –
a fizzy drink made
from hoobnips

Hooboblubbers – delicious puddings

Hoobysandwichhammer – a special hammer used to whack cheese sandwiches (Hoobs like their sandwiches nice and flat!)

Here's a hooby hello from
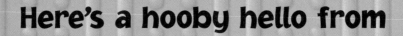
"Hoobledoop! Hoobledoop! Whoop! Whoop! Whoop!"

"Hoobledoop Tiddlypeeps. I'm Tula. I have pink hoobyfur, a green twizzletuft and a green nose. I'm pretty clever and I have lots of good ideas for making things."

A fantabihooby picture of Tula for you to colour.

Hoobygalooby! Here it is!
THE HOOBMOBILE
The hoobygrooviest way to travel!

The Hoobmobile takes the Hoobs anywhere they want to go. It's bright and colourful and reminds them of Hoobland. On top is a roof garden filled with strange, hoobashious plants. It has lots of peepholes and portholes, as well as a balcony and a tiny door. And the engine is powered by the musical Motorettes –

Tootle, Twang and Timp!!

Colour in this picture of the Hoobmobile using your most hoobashious colours.

FANCY DRESS

One day, inside the Hoobmobile ...

The Hoobs were getting ready for a Tiddlypeep fancy dress party! "Hoobledoobledooper!" said Tula. "I know what I'm going to be!" And inside her hoobybitz box she found everything she needed to make her costume. "Aaaark!" she squawked. "Look at me! I'm a hoobyholler bird!"

"Will the Tiddlypeeps know what a hoobyholler bird is?" said Iver, sensibly. Tula decided to ask them.

"Help!" cried the Tiddlypeeps when they saw Tula. "It's a monster!" "I'm not a monster!" she said, sadly. "I'm a hoobyholler bird!" "You look too scary!" said the Tiddlypeeps. "You'd better choose another costume."

So Tula went back to the Hoobmobile to think again...

"What shall we wear to a fancy dress party?"

THINK SONG

When you're stuck for
an answer
Or what to do
STOP
Hmmmmmmm
Think it through!

Take a deep breath in
Think it out
Work it through
Don't **scream** and **shout**

Think it through
Don't go **boo hoo**
Think it through
You'll feel brand new
If you think it through
If you think it **through!**

39

Just then, Hubba Hubba appeared on the hoobycomputer screen and told the Hoobs a story...

Wanda the witch was fed up. Every year she entered the Great Broomstick Race, and every year she came last!

"Maybe I'm too heavy," she thought. So she stopped eating bat burgers and went to a keep-fit class. But some of the exercises were impossible to do in a witch's hat!

"Maybe I need a new broomstick!" she thought. So she went to her local broomstick shop and asked the shopkeeper for the fastest broomstick in the world.

"That's the Supersonic Sweeper," replied the shopkeeper. "But I sold the last one to Wizard Whizzy!"

Wanda went home feeling even more fed up. Then she had an idea! The answer was inside her kitchen cupboard. "Yes!" she cried, excitedly. "A quick magic spell and I will have the best Supersonic Sweeper ever!"

At midnight, the wizards and witches lined up at the start of the Great Broomstick Race. And there was Wanda, sitting on her magic vacuum cleaner!

"Ready, steady, go!" Wanda shot into the distance and zoomed over the finishing line before anyone else had got as far as the first chimney pot.

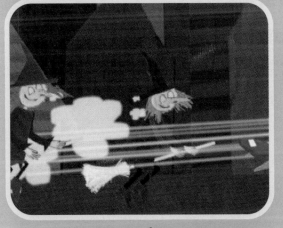

"Hooray!" said Wanda. At last she was the winner and she was the happiest witch in the world.

THE END

Iver and Groove enjoyed Hubba Hubba's story so much that they decided to go to the party dressed as wizards.

"We can make wizardy wands from my collection of long pointy things!" said Groove, excitedly.

But Tula wasn't so happy. "How do I look dressed as a witch?" she asked.

"Hoobashious!" said Iver. "You make a really ugly witch, Tula!"

"Oh, but I want to look pretty!" she moaned. "I'll have to think again..."

Just then, Roma appeared on the hoobycomputer screen with her daily news report.

"Hoobledoop, Hoobs!" she began. "I'm on a farm and

I've found something that the Peeps call a scarecrow. It keeps the birds away from the farmer's seeds."

"That's it!" said Groove. "We'll make you a scarecrow costume, Tula!" But Tula felt even sadder dressed in old scarecrow clothes.

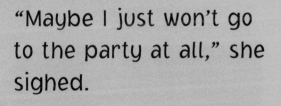

"Maybe I just won't go to the party at all," she sighed.

"Don't give up!" said Groove. "Let's ask the Tiddlypeeps. They always have an answer... "

Tula explained her problem to the Tiddlypeeps. "My hooby holler bird costume was too scary," she said. "My witch's costume was too ugly, and my scarecrow costume was too sad! I want to go to the party feeling happy. Can you help?"

"Yes, we can!" said the Tiddlypeeps, putting a sparkly tiara on Tula's head.

"Oh, hoobygalooby!" said Tula. "That makes me feel pretty already!" And before long Tula was dressed as a beautiful, magical fairy.

"I feel as if I could fly!" she said.

Now all the Hoobs were happy and ready for the party.

"Hoob hoob hooray!"

She'll be coming to the party when she comes!
She'll be coming to the party when she comes!
She'll be coming to the party
Coming to the party
Coming to the party when she comes!

She'll be dressed up as a fairy when she comes!
She'll be dressed up as a fairy when she comes!
She'll be dressed up as a fairy
Dressed up as a fairy
Dressed up as fairy when she comes!

Timp, Twang and Tootle love to make up songs.
Can you make up some more verses for this song?

A HOOBY PUZZLE

These Tiddlypeeps are going to the fancy dress party.
Which hat belongs with which costume?

Here's a hooby hello from
ROMA
"Hoobledoop! Hoobledoop!
Whoop! Whoop! Whoop!"

"Hoobledoop Tiddlypeeps. I'm Roma – the roving Hoob news reporter. I have orange hoobyfur, a pink twizzletuft and a pink nose. I'm fearless and I will go anywhere for a good piece of news!"

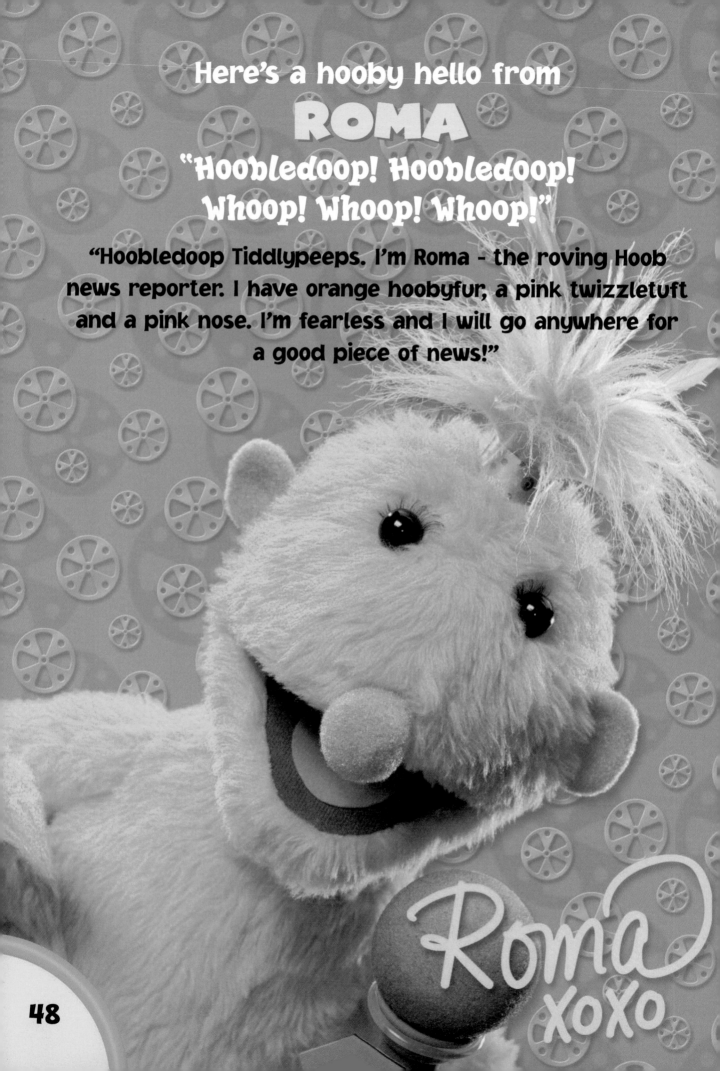

Roma
xoxo

48

A hoobygroovy picture of Roma for you to colour.

One day, on top of the Hoobmobile ...

Groove was dusting the plants when he came to his favourite Peep tree and noticed something different.
"What's happened to your green leaves?" he asked the tree. "They've gone all brown and crispy!" Tula and Iver came to see.

"Oh, dear," said Tula, "your tree must be feeling sad."
Then Groove tried dusting the tree and some of the leaves fell off!
"My poor tree will soon be naked!" he cried.

"Maybe we can stick them back on with hoobofix," suggested Iver. But, back inside the Hoobmobile, the leaves just wouldn't stick. Then Hubba Hubba's face appeared on the hoobycomputer screen. "This is an important question for my Hoobopaedia," he said.

Why do trees lose their leaves?

"Why? Why? Why?" sang the Motorettes.

Hubba Hubba found some pictures of trees on the Hoobnet...

"Well," said Groove, feeling happier, "at least my tree isn't the only one losing its leaves. I'll ask the Tiddlypeeps if they know why... "

The Tiddlypeeps were
making leaf prints.
"Is that why the leaves
fall off the trees, so that
you can have fun with
them?" asked Groove.
"No," laughed the Tiddlypeeps, "the trees lose their
leaves because it's autumn!"
"Autumn!" repeated Groove. "I see. What's autumn?"

"It's a time of year, when it
gets colder and the leaves
change colour and fall off
the trees," they explained.
"Thank you," said Groove,
and he rushed to tell the
others.

Just then, Hubba Hubba found a story for the
Hoobs...

There was once a happy tree called Cyril Sycamore. In the summer he liked to stretch out his branches and wave his beautiful green leaves in the warm breeze.

In the autumn, when the days grew shorter and the air grew colder, Cyril's leaves turned red, orange, brown and gold. Then, one by one, they fluttered to the ground.

Cyril loved the autumn because his leaves turned such beautiful colours and tickled when they blew off in the wind.

He liked to play a game, trying to guess which leaf would hit the ground first.

When autumn turned to winter and it was very, very, cold, Cyril would relax his roots and drift off into a deep, peaceful sleep.

And while he was asleep, he would happily dream of spring, when he could wake up and grow some fresh, green leaves.

THE END

"Hoobygalooby!" whooped Groove, when he had listened to the story. "My tree is going to sleep for the winter!"

"Shsshh!" whispered Iver. "Your tree won't be able to sleep if you make such a noise."

Just then, Roma appeared on the hoobycomputer
screen.

"Hoobledoop, Hoobs!"
she said. "I'm reporting from
the other side of the world!
And guess what! Here it is
spring and all the trees are
growing new green leaves! And soon it will be
summer. And then autumn, then winter, then back to
spring again. These are called seasons."
"That's hoobygroovy!" said Groove. "So all I have to
do is wait until spring and then my tree will grow
new leaves!"

"This Peep planet is full
of surprises!" said Tula.
"I wonder what I would
look like if I lost *my*
hoobyfur in the winter!"
said Groove.
"Yeeeegh!" laughed the
others!

A HOOBY PUZZLE

Groove has been busy building a hoobashious snowman. But who does it look like?
Join the dots to find out.

Here's a hooby hello from
HUBBA HUBBA
"Hoobledoop! Hoobledoop! Whoop! Whoop! Whoop!"

"Hoobledoop Tiddlypeeps. I'm Hubba Hubba. I have blue hoobyfur, hoobashious blue ears and an orange nose! I live in Hoobland where I am compiling my great Hoobopaedia. I like to keep an eye on the Hoobs and help them with their mission."

A hoobelly groobelly picture of Hubba Hubba for you to colour.

HOOBSPEAK!

Want to speak like the HOOBS?
Then look it up here in the totally hoobashious Hoob Dictionary!

HOOBLEDOOP! Hello!

HOOBLETOODLEDOO!
Goodbye!

HoobyGALOOBY!
Wow!

Hoob! Hoob! HOORAY!
Hip Hip Hooray!

HOOBLEDOOBLEDOOPER Super!

HoobyGROOVY
Really Cool!

HOOBASHIOUS Marvellous!

HOOBELLY GROOBELLY Lovely!
FANTABIHOOBY Truly fantastic!

HOOBWORDS!

HOOBS
furry, inquisitive creatures from Hoobland

HOOBOPAEDIA
a database of everything Hoobs would want to know. Hoobs all over the universe are collecting information for this

HOOBMOBILE
the Hoobs fantastic musical bus

TWIZZLETUFT
the fluffy topknot on a Hoob's head

HOOBLEDIGGER
a special hooby hug

HOOBNET   the web

HOOBYBOOBOO   a mistake

HOOBYPODS   what Hoobs sleep in

PEEP PLANET   the world

PEEPS   grown-ups

TIDDLYPEEPS   children

WRINKLY PEEP   old person

SQUIGGLYTIDDLYPEEPS   babies